THE POETIC ART
OF SEDUCTION

~VOLUME 3~

By
Clarissa O. Clemens

Clarissa O. Clemens

ISBN-10: 061587438X

ISBN-13: 978-0615874388

Pleasure Portal Press

Table of Contents

Angles of Arousal 12

Hard to Resist 13

Ponytail Reins...14

Unhinged 15

Passion to Please 17

Sticky Schemes 18

Love Knot 19

10, 11, 12 22

Take Me to the Extreme 23

Sensing You 25

Fantasies Found 27

Pilot of My Fantasies..29

Heart First into Bliss 30

Checkmate 32

Aching for the Quaking...34

Pending Penetration 36

Shower Scene..37

Sweet Seductive Game 39

Euphoria Exposed 40

Between His Thighs 42

A Breath of Lust...43

Take the Plunge **44**

Rambunctious Rendezvous................................**46**

Thighs of Desire **48**

Unzipped Door **50**

Cascading Words **53**

Hello lovers of erotic words…
My hope is that by reading my poetry you will feel the passion and playfulness of your own sensuality and be able to use my writings to add some spice to your love life.

Thank you so much for your support!

Seductively Yours,
Clarissa

P.S – All online reviews are greatly welcomed and appreciated xo

Be sure to check out my other volumes of passionate poetry available worldwide at all online and on-ground bookstores –

The Poetic Art of Seduction, Volume 1
The Poetic Art of Seduction, Volume 2
The Poetic Diary of Love and Change, Volume 1
The Poetic Diary of Love and Change, Volume 2

Find me on Twitter - @clarissaclemens

Visit my playful & sexy website -
www.pleasureportalpress.com

Listen to me read my poems on YouTube
http://www.youtube.com/user/ClarissaClemens

Angles of Arousal

His angles of arousal
Melt her curves of desire
With locks loose and tousled
Peering at his need, she conspires
Straight up yet slanted
Pointing in her direction of pleasure
Mesmerized and enchanted
Every move calculated and measured
With preciseness and cunning
He eyes her assets and talents
Curvaceous-ness tumbles into stunning
The sight of her tips him off balance
He grabs a handful of her squeeze-to-please
She has the power of the titillating tease
He licks his lips in longing anticipation
Smoothly she mounts his standing ovation
Riding relentless his rigidness succumbs
Tightly she grips him until he fights not to come
Deep inside of her he is helpless to his urges
Thrusting within her. his body shudders as it merges
They begin to move in unison, rhythmically as one
The avalanche of tingles is about to come undone
Their eyes connect
Their fingers intersect
They know they have reached
Their passionate peak
With waves of wonder wielding its power
The angle of arousal
Has been fully devoured

Hard to Resist

Super steamy creamy yum
Dripping off my eager tongue
Savor flavor kept inside
Enjoying the taste, feeling it glide
Swallow slowly down my throat
Sensory overload making me float
Ready steady more is coming
Body on fire, desire humming
Soft to touch, hard to resist
A lick of luscious, a flick of the wrist
Encourages more to flow to the top
Guiding the rhythm, controlling the pop
Slowing the action for maximum satisfaction
Speeding it up to gain tactile traction
Teasingly squeezing, caressing, and pleasing
Easing it in no longer teasing
Twisting and turning, churning and yearning
Sliding it down, feeling you burning
Deeper and deeper, I keep you held
Releasing the tension, together we meld
Swollen and aching
Begging and quaking
Eruption of passion
Shiver and shaking
You take what you need,
everything you require
Dismounting the steed
Fulfilled and inspired

Ponytail Reins

Ponytail reins
To grip and restrain
He grabs and guides
To take the ride
Pulling her in
A devilish grin
Sliding inside
Their hips collide
Forcing her back
Tickle and smack
Pleasant surprise
Drips down her thighs
He yanks her close
The passion flows
Between their flanks
Ready for spanks
Under his thumb
Her body does hum
Slippery slack
Losing track
He wraps her hair
As if in a snare
She can't get away
Holding his prey
With one last move
Their hips
In a groove
Into the bliss
Of submissiveness

Unhinged

Hanging dangling
Balls of joy
Fondling fingering
Your jewel-laden toys
Cream engorged heat
Your most precious treats
Delving underneath
The slippery sheets
I find your thickness
Invites my quickness
Stroke the slickness
With satisfying swiftness
Diving beneath
I explore your sheath

Always my tongue
Barely my teeth
Running my kiss
Lips full of bliss
Along your length
Girth, warmth, and strength
Your need for release
Pulls me in tighter to please
My breath ragged and panting
Allowing you the pleasure I am granting
My touch tingles and taunts
I have you exactly where I want
Just one more small move
You become unhinged from your groove
Erratic ecstatic traumatic emphatic
Swallowing succulent streams of cream
I possess your mess the success I caress

Passion to Please

Passion to please
Squeeze and tease
On my knees
Swaying in the breeze
Waiting for you to seize
Control of me
Hearing the tone
And command of your voice
Telling me it is time
To let go of all choice
I am here for you
To take your pleasure
Wrapped up in your arms
A quivering treasure
A handful of hair
Your penetrating stare
The melted state
That you create
Leaves us breathless
Sensations endless
We float together
Tightly fettered
Riding our seduction
Without interruption
To bring you to that place
Where all thoughts are erased

Sticky Schemes

Spread and sprawl
Explore and crawl
Search and saunter
Pry and ponder

Dark and deep
Take a peek
Invite and enter
Tight and tighter

Long and thick
Shiny and slick
Enters within
Makes the room spin

Stir and stab
Lick and grab
Whipped creamy dreams
Sticky sensuous schemes

Love Knot

Sleep sweet
Dream wild
Chills tingle
Erotic style

Move fluid
Swerving rhythm
Side to side
Hypnotic vision

Tease touch
Wind blowing
Whispered hush
Mind flowing

Embraced tight
Skin silky
Lips light
Breathless sultry

Pressed firm
Conforming shapes
Meld and squirm
Thoughts escape

Love breathes
Souls merge
Volition leaves
Emotions surge

Lusciously linked
Without thought
Hearts interlinked
Love knot

10, 11, 12

Spankings end the day
In a resounding way
Bent over knees
A smack meant to please
Bare hand to flesh
Cheeks red and flushed
Stinging with stimulation
Firm cause and duration
She counts the impact,
when hand meets skin
Restrained yet restless,
with wrists firmly pinned
Ten, then eleven, and next comes twelve
Into subspace she tumbles dizzy and resolved
Intoxicated by pain
Pleasure close and sustained
One more, then a rub
A loving Dom treats his sub
To his will, her desire
Mutual respect that inspires
Bending to his need
Her volition is freed
He will take her gift
See the power shift
From his heart to her trust
Together they combust

Take Me to the Extreme

Spread me
Melt me
Make me scream

Suck me
Bite me
Taste my cream

Lick me
Love me
Be my dream

Find me
Hold me
See me beam

Probe me
Pry me
Deep and obscene

Tie me
Bind me
Pleasures seen

Take me
Use me
Sexual scene

Grip me
Grind me
Hear me sing

Thrust me
Lust me
Take me to the Extreme

Sate me
Fill me
Floating Serene

Sensing You

The sweet smell of success

Is dripping
down
your leg

The tantalizing taste of your lure

Is sticking
to
my tongue

The virile view of your passion

Pulls
relentlessly
at my heart

The sensuous sound of your voice

Keeps me
alert and
moist

The tender touch that grazes my soul

Has the deepest
and tightest
hold

The way you stroke my senses

Puts me
under
Your
complete
and total
Control

Fantasies Found

Poke me
Stroke me
Call out my name

Drive me inward
Drive me insane

Unbuttoned
Unzipped
Licking the whip

Tasting the cream
Satisfying trip

Luxurious tactile
Tantalizing touch

Wondrous wanderings
A quiet hush

Facets of fulfillment
Fluttering inside

Waiting for culmination
Ready for the ride

Moan and groan
Let out the grind

Exposing buried fantasies
We eagerly find

With all wishes granted
Sensual dreams come true

All limits are expanded
A delectable delicious view

My partner in passion
We harness the beast

Whatever we can imagine
Will become our feast

Pilot of My Fantasies

You are the pilot of my fantasies
Steering me away from reality
Made of images we create in our minds
Leading us towards the wildness we can find
Together we explore all realms of being
Sensual yet kinky but totally freeing
Trust that binds us allows for sharing
All ideas pondered our intimacy baring
Expression lands us raw and intense
Ideas unlocked excitingly immense
So many situations and fun to try out
Partners of pleasure no limits no doubt
Flying high on accumulated clouds of delight
Fanning the flame of your pilot light
I am the co-pilot to your dreams of extreme
Spreading our wings following our schemes
Making the visions we held in our head
Come alive and play out landing in our bed

Heart First into Bliss

Soaring slippery
Isles of flesh
Meshed together
Interlocked and refreshed
Languorous lavish loving limbs
Tapping timeless thoughts and whims
Embraced so tight
Lips locked flush
Tingling tactile
Tantalizing touch
Sparks of passion
Fuel my actions
On my knees
So ready to please
Parked in seduction
Trying to function
Perfectly placed
Passionate kiss
Leaning and lunging,
Heart first into bliss

Checkmate

Slinking around
With sex at my side
Crawling into thoughts
Massaging my mind
Juices begin to flow
Ideas start to leak
Lips start to part
I begin to speak
Touching stroking
Caressing in sips
Skin so silky
Curves slide past fingertips
Sensuous songs
Urging me on
I see your castle
I move my pawn
Enter the realm
Of breathless words
Hearing the melody
Of singing birds
Maneuvers positioning
Bodies in line
Watching your eyes
Looking for a sign

The sparkle in your eye
Is telling me why
I need to relinquish
And follow the wish
Of being together
If only forever
When I check, you are my mate

Aching for the Quaking

Each cheek spread
And slightly red
Awaiting the next move
Restrained in your bed

The toys lined up
And ready to go
The swish of the flogger
To and fro

Aching for the quaking
Under your command
Lifting my limbs
Upon your demand

Anxious for spanks
Stinging the supple flanks
Of my rear endeared
And under your hand

The power and strength
Towers over my meekness
The girth and length
Never betrays your weakness

For my flesh soft and smooth
As you fall into your groove
Each movement fluid
Finding me awake yet more lucid

I accept what you deliver
With a flinch then a shiver
Of delight and lust
Trusting your final thrust

Bringing us closer to ecstasy
Bonded together in love and intimacy

Pending Penetration

Hard protuberance
Pending penetration
Brushes my morning
Electrifying sensation
Into soft wet folds
Snugly we mold
Eagerly awaiting
Taunting and baiting
Churning and cherishing
Modesty perishing
Throbbing erect
Swollen flesh connects
His breath in my ear
Straddling his spear
Keep the beat of the heat
Slipping against sheets
Strong and rhythmic
Pumping in time
Our heartbeats in sync
Our bodies so primed
The best way to start a day
So erotic, so divine

Shower Scene

Soapy and wet
Anticipating yet
Slippery to get
Inside your holes
Letting go of control
Pleasure our goal
Showerhead pulses
Shutters and convulses
Against our flesh

With our limbs tightly meshed
Warm and dreamy
Seductive and steamy
Breath at your neck
A kiss then a peck
Fingers slide quickly
Slithering and slick
Building urges
Stiffness emerges
Swollen heat
Grabbing for your meat
Position bent
Parted to relent
Spread and open
Intentions unspoken
Wetness in and out
Our climax starts to spout
Tiles cool against palms
Waves rise and then calm
Clean serene clutching tight
Naughty scene an elegant sight

Sweet Seductive Game

I want to be the marshmallow
Impaled on your skewer
I want you to pollinate
My succulent flower
I want to be the nectar
Melting over your flame
I want to know all the rules of this
Sweet seductive game
I want to feel my openness
As it is filled with your joy
I want to hear your passion please
Tickle my ear with your noise
I need to inhale your manliness
Primal primed prim and ready
Your scent sends my over the edge
Teetering unsteady
I need to feel the power
Of your body and mind
I need to release all tensions
A sensual unwind
I need to know that you want me and
You'll always be mine

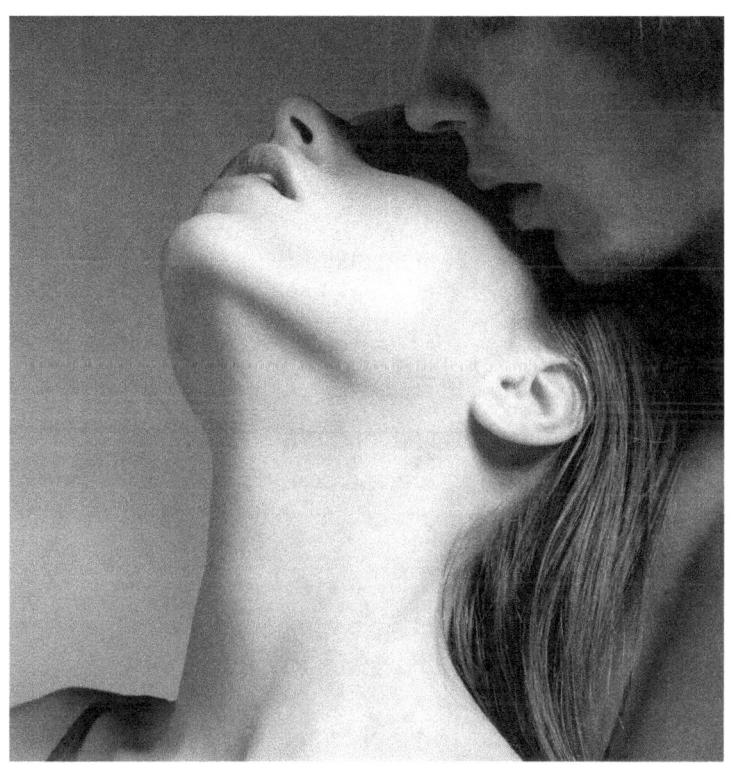

Euphoria Exposed

Dizzy on the ground
If we were not lying down
We would fall endlessly
From the euphoria we have found

With the taste of his sweetness
Still in her mouth
Breathless and speechless
Floating on a cloud

Thankful for the floor
Contemplating more
Rising up swaying
and locking the door

Regain stability
One foot ahead
Back to the comfort
and pleasures in our bed

Rolling connected meshing our souls
Controlling and dominating
Assuming our roles

Exposed, we dance
On sheets swimming in lust
Wrists and ankles tangled up in trust

Swirling pheromones
Sub-space in place
The look of nirvana
Glowing from her face

He gently holds her in his arms
Secured in the heat of his body and charms
He wraps his heart around her wants
She encircles herself around his response

Between His Thighs

Grabbing between
His parted thighs
Induces shudders
and heavy sighs
Feather soft kisses
Trail and tease
Peeking from behind
Bent and knackered knees
Gazing upward
Toward his erected tower
Feeling the nectar dripping down
the petals of my flower
His eyes aglow
With anticipatory glory
Scooped up in his arms
In a rapid fury
Muscles ripple
With intent to conquer
Waves of passion
Cascade and capture
Avalanche of emotion
Collides between us
Explosive eruption
Plunging deep into
Dreamy unconsciousness

A Breath of Lust

When I exhale
My sex fills the room
When I lift the veil
My thoughts are consumed
A cloud of looming lust
Settles over our beings
Permeated and hushed
Electric waves of feeling
their way through my veins
Charging with tingles
Pulling on my chain
Our energy commingles
Arms of arousal
Legs interlocked
Intimate proposal
Heads are cocked
Fingertips probing
Opens vulnerability
Stiffness invites stroking
Sliding so rhythmically
Breathing in lust
Deep into our lungs
Embracing your trust
Tangling into each other's tongues
Intoxicated and dizzy
Swirling in a lovers haze
Light-headed and spinning
Your gaze all ablaze
Inhale the vapors
A sensuous potpourri
Most delicious of scents
Come breathe it in with me

Take the Plunge

Push pull
Grab full
Hips swerve
Sumptuous curves
Bend and bind
Throbbing from behind
Spank and yank
Walking the plank
To take the plunge
Arch and lunge
Totally submerged
Lust-filled surge
In out
Beyond a doubt
The movement felt
Bodies will melt
Together pooled
Heat that cools
Sizzling touch
A gasp a hush
Deep shallow
Suck and swallow
Nectar flows
Hunger grows
Pulsing and pleasing
Swollen yet easing
Inside your mine
On passions we dine

Rambunctious Rendezvous

Entering slowly
on a quest for the prize
Planning my move
staring into your eyes
Steamy and sticky
poised on the perch
Raunchy and ready
going on a search
I have you kneeling
waiting for my command
Sweetly submissive
pleasure on demand
Head lowered
locks amiss
Buns warming
waiting for a kiss
Stockings inched up
accentuating hips
Lovely sex sauce
oozes and drips
Scooping up your melons
juicy and sweet
Licking the sweetness
sliding into your heat
Dipping and tantalizing
teasing and squeezing
Rambunctious rendezvous
ready for seizing
Tweaking titillating
tips of nips
Gyrating undulating

licking your lips
A nibble nudging
beneath your need
Between my teeth
trapping your bead
Separating mounds
parting your holes
You have no choice
but to release control
Tongue darting deeper with each stroke
Fingers prying and probing to poke
Extracting your honey
hearing your pleas
Begging and whimpering
asking for release
I give you your reward
only after I am done
Exploring your body
is half the fun
Mercy and satisfaction
are coming your way
Grabbing your hips
you start to sway
You understand the time
has come for your reward
To let go of the simmer
you have stored
Deep in your body
ready to explode
One touch from him
And the waves implode
Shattering shackles crumpling together
Languid and spent, letting go of the pressure

Thighs of Desire

Long lovely legs
leading to lust
Spread and straining
yearning for his thrust
Straddling silky
smooth thighs of desire
Skirt hiked up
a little bit higher
Panties framing
the sweetness of hips

Each edge lowered down
with a nibbling kiss
Sliding seductively
first one leg then the other
With a flick of her toe
she is now fully uncovered
A glance towards his rise
signals the next move
His belt is unbuckled
and his jeans are removed
Warm hands and fingers
fondle and caress
As they view each other
now completely undressed
Naked and vulnerable
inside and out
Open and waiting
no longer able to holdout
Their lips link up
Tongues twirl in a dance
Passion erupting
heads blurred in a trance
Slippery sliding
swollen and erect
Dizzy and panting
their bodies intersect
One undulating mass of motion
Sparks and moans
culminate in explosion
Her long lovely legs
lay limp from exhaustion

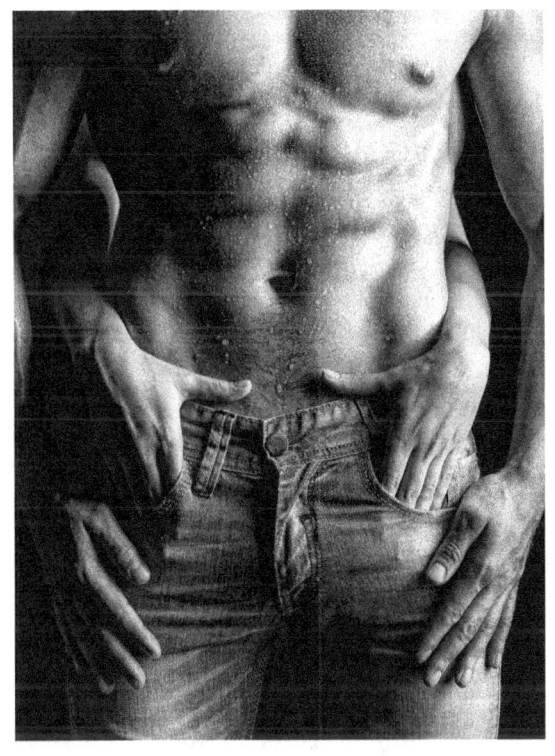

Unzipped Door

Your open fly is a silent cry
for me
to set you free

Inviting enticing luring me in
to taste the icing
off your heated skin

Fabric that folds and flippantly flaunts
Accentuating and caressing
your bulging taunt

Edging closer fingertips explore
Prying wide open your
unzipped door

Metal buckle, leather strap
loosened and flopping
setting my trap

Fingers inch in to find what I want
Maneuvering your meat
Acting nonchalant

Eased out and ready
throbbing with your need
taking control of your pulsing steed

Dabbling playful handful expands
sliding around
your magnificent demand

Musky man smell excites my senses
entranced by the dance
as you let down your defenses

The contrast and feel
of your jeans against warm flesh
movement and rhythm link and intermesh

The taste and the feel
as your nectar drips out
leaves no doubt that I must let him out

Building your urgency with absolute certainty
stroking and licking
ever so fervently

Slow and wet, I know exactly what I will get
If I keep up the beat
I will receive my treat

Feeling the eruption
jetting up to blow
I position myself to lap up your flow

Every thrust sends you deeper inside
Swallowing skillfully
I slip and glide

Your waves of passion
propel me on a ride
emptying your load until it subsides

Sliding happiness back into your pants
flaccid and spent
thoroughly content

The zipper reluctantly closes tight
with your taste in my mouth
sweetness and light

For My Love of Poetry

Cascading Words

Tucked in the corner
of my imaginative mind

Possibilities explode
when freed from behind

The opportunities wanting
and waiting to be ceased

Won't leave me alone
won't be appeased

Until I grab them

they make me their pawn

Tickling my creativity
egging me on

Erupting in splendor
Dazzling with joy

Skyrocket my heart
Ready to rejoice

Words cascading
and deliciously strewn

Lines of passion
Feeling my heart swoon

With deeply felt sensations
transcribed from within

Sharing my love for life
The lines fall out and begin

Lyrical and choreographed
In a unique and beautiful dance

Relinquished, embraced,
and under a poetic trance

Clarissa O. Clemens